"WHEN" "PAPA" "SNORES"

by *Melinda Long*

pictures by *Holly Meade*

Simon & Schuster

Books for Young Readers

New York London Toronto Sydney Singapore

Nana says that sometimes Papa snores.

And Papa says that sometimes Nana snores.

The truth is, they both snore.
I just can't decide who snores louder.

When Papa snores,

HONNKK

SHOOOOO

HONNKK

SHOOOOO. . .

the lamp at his bedside rattles and shakes.

When Nana snores,

CARRROOSH . . . CARRROOSH

the blinds on the window clink-clank together.

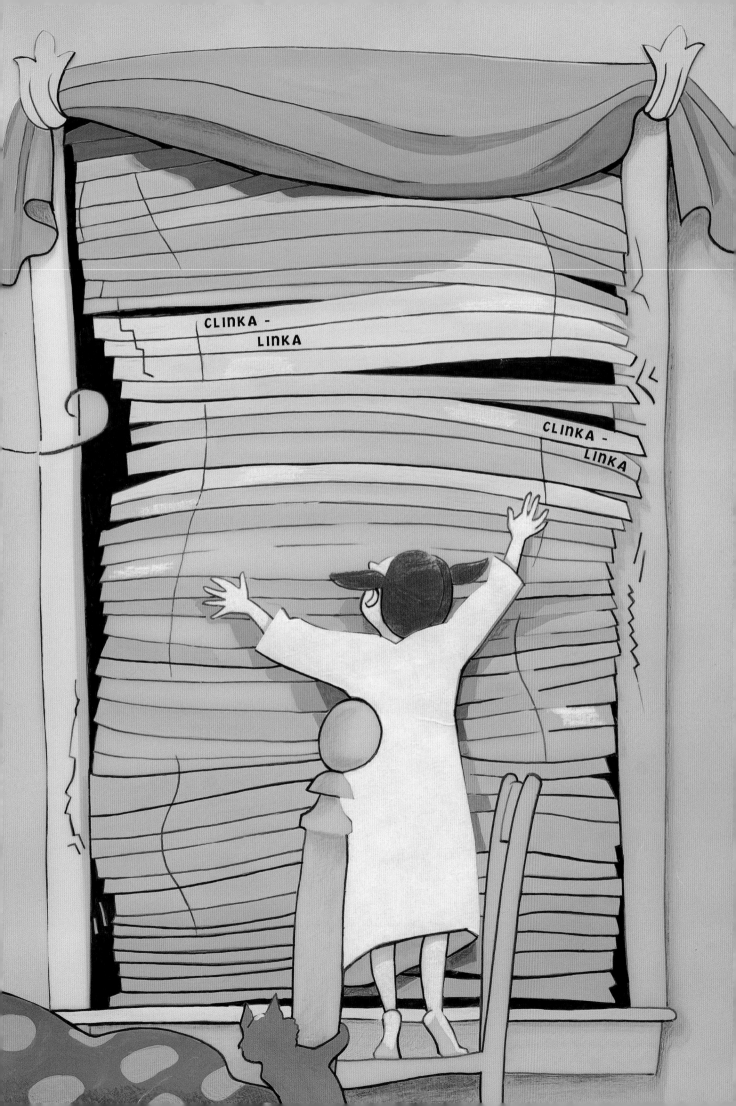

When Papa snores,

ARRGHH-OOOMM

. . . ARRGHH-OOOMM

the lamp at his bedside rattles and shakes,
and the drawers of his dresser
open and close.

When Nana snores,
GARRUUM . . . GARRUUM

the blinds on the window
clink-clank together, and the dishes
in the drainer shake themselves dry.

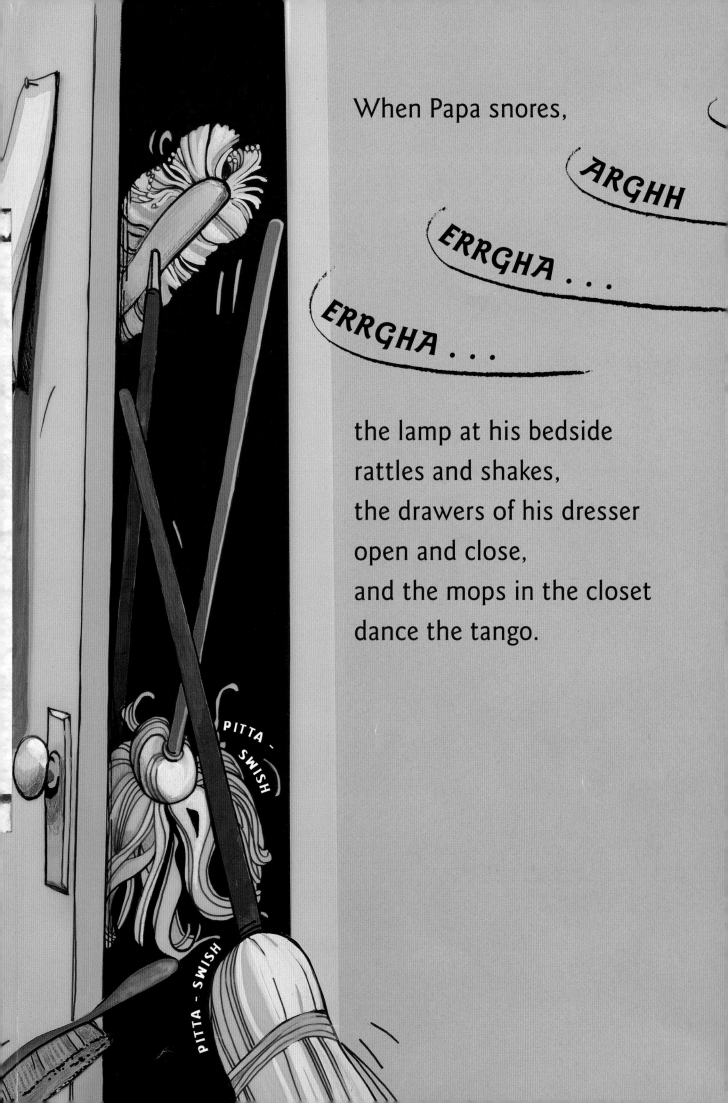

When Papa snores,

the lamp at his bedside
rattles and shakes,
the drawers of his dresser
open and close,
and the mops in the closet
dance the tango.

When Nana snores,

SNOOOOGA . . .

SNOOOOGA . . .

SNOOM

the blinds on the window clink-clank together,
the dishes in the drainer shake themselves dry,
and the limbs on the trees throw their leaves
to the ground.

When Papa snores,

SCURRAFFFA TAFFA TAF

the lamp at his bedside rattles and shakes,
the drawers of his dresser open and close,
the mops in the closet dance the tango,
and the manhole covers bounce down the street.

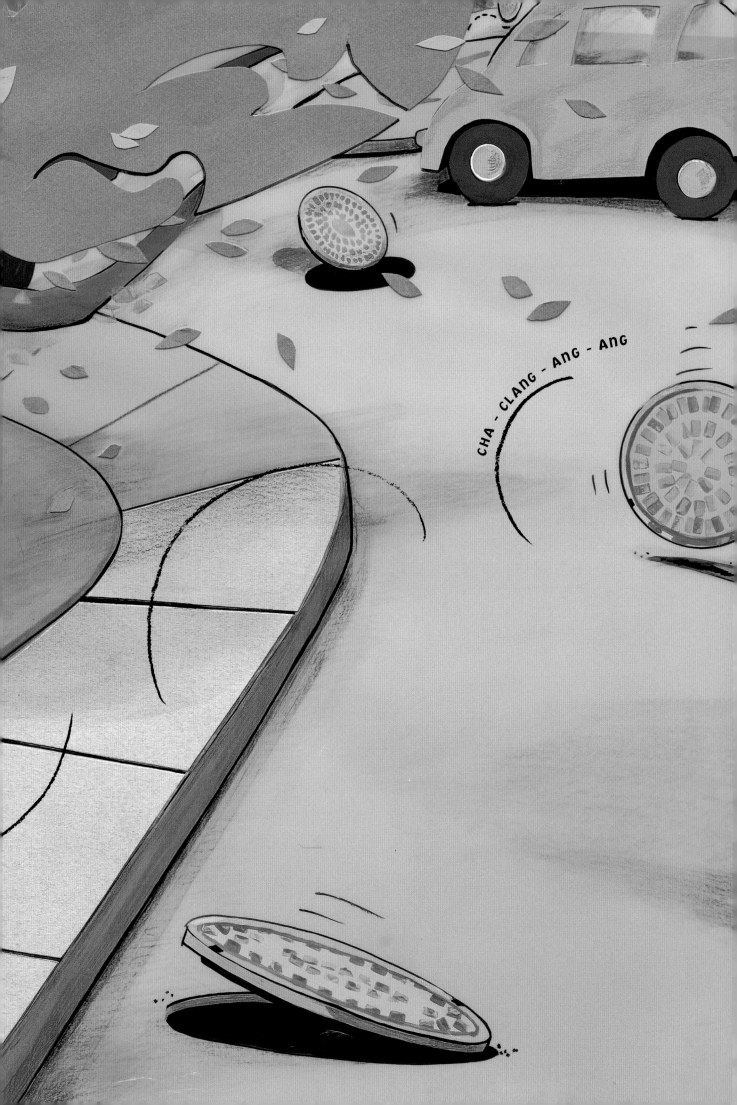

When Nana snores,
GIDDA-GIDDA-GIDDA-IDDA

the blinds on the window clink-clank together,
the dishes in the drainer shake themselves dry,
the limbs on the trees throw their leaves
to the ground,
and the shoes on the shoe rack tumble down
the stairs.

I'm not sure who's louder, but my mom says that when Nana and Papa snore at the same time, the people in the next state sit up in bed and yell,
"Quiet out there!
We're trying to get some rest!"

CUUURRRSHUMMMM ....

Mama says that nobody can sleep
when the two of them snore.
And Mama is almost always right
about everything.

But not this time . . . (yawn).
'Cause when Nana and Papa snore,
it sounds just like (yawn) music to me.
And I feel safe (yawn) and sound (yawn). . .
and sleepy (yawn).

M - m - m - m - m - m . . .

(sigh) good night.

SNORT, HONKITY - SHNOO - SHNOOO
RISH - ROOSH
TEKKA - TEKKA
TINK - A - TINK
SHIRR - CLOP
PUDDITY - PUD

SNORT, HONKITY - SHNOO - SHNOOOO
THWAP - THWAP
WHEE - UUM
RISH - ROOSH
PUR-R-R-R-R-R
RIFFA
RIFFA
RIFFA

For Thom, who knows how snoring really sounds,
and for Cathy and Bryan, who always laugh at my stories —M.L.

AUTHOR'S ACKNOWLEDGMENTS
My sincere gratitude goes to Steven Malk for seeing potential where others
saw just another writer, and to Stephanie Owens Lurie
for showing me how to make a story become a book.

SIMON & SCHUSTER BOOKS FOR YOUNG READERS
An imprint of Simon & Schuster Children's Publishing Division
1230 Avenue of the Americas, New York, New York 10020
Text copyright © 2000 by Melinda Long
Illustrations copyright © 2000 by Holly Meade
The board game, Mouse Trap, depicted on page 2 is used with permission.
MOUSETRAP® is a trademark of Hasbro, Inc. © 2000 Hasbro, Inc.
All rights reserved including the right of reproduction in whole or in part in any form.
SIMON & SCHUSTER BOOKS FOR YOUNG READERS is a trademark of Simon & Schuster.
Book design by Chris Hammill Paul
The text of this book is set in 21-point Goudy Sans.
The illustrations are rendered in gouache and ink with some cut paper.
Printed in Hong Kong
2   4   6   8   10   9   7   5   3   1

LIBRARY OF CONGRESS CATALOGING-IN-PUBLICATION DATA

Long, Melinda.
When Papa snores / by Melinda Long ; illustrated by Holly Meade.—1st ed.
p.   cm.
Summary: A child describes the increasing intensity of her grandparents'
snores—that annoy some but also provide a sense of security.
ISBN 0-689-81943-9 (hc.)
[1. Snoring—Fiction. 2. Grandparents—Fiction.] I. Meade, Holly, ill. II. Title.
PZ7.L856Wh 2000
98-24121   CIP   AC

first
edition